For Ella – KU
For all my nephews and nieces – AC

The Sophie Rabbit Books:
Sophie and Abigail
Sophie and the wonderful picture
Sophie and the Mother's Day card
Sophie in charge

This edition published in the UK 2005 by
Mathew Price Limited
The Old Glove Factory, Bristol Road
Sherborne, Dorset DT9 4HP
Text copyright © Kaye Umansky 1995
Illustrations copyright © Anna Currey 1995
Edited by Belinda Hollyer

ISBN 1-84248-126-6

Printed in China

Sophie in charge

Kaye Umansky
Sophie in charge

Illustrated by Anna Currey

MATHEW PRICE LIMITED

Sophie Rabbit's school was holding a summer fair.

WELCOME TO BRIARY INFANTS' SUMMER FAYRE! said the poster.

Everywhere was hustle and bustle.

There were stalls selling cakes,
plants, books and home-made jam.
There was a Lucky Dip, a Roundabout,
and a Bouncy Mushroom. There was a
Coconut Shy, and a Hook-the-Duck game.

Sophie's mum was on the cake stall.

"Keep your eye on Gareth for me, love," she said. "I can't sell cakes and watch him at the same time. I'd need eyes in the top of my ears!"

"Can't Dad?" said Sophie.

"Dad's not coming till later. He'll be good, won't you, Gareth?"

"NO," said Gareth cheerfully. It was his new word. He said it a lot.

"All right," said Sophie. She held out her paw. "Come on, Gareth."

Immediately, Gareth put on one of his naughty looks.

"NO!" he said. And ran off, as fast as his little legs would carry him.

For a rabbit who had only just learnt to walk, that was very fast indeed. The trouble was, he giggled so much he didn't look where he was going, and ran head first into the Lucky Dip.

"Woah! Steady on there, young feller!" said Trevor Otter's dad, who was in charge. "You've got your paws full there, young Sophie."

"I know," sighed Sophie.

Mrs Squirrel was in charge of Hook-the-Duck. There was a long queue, but Gareth didn't bother with things like queues. He went straight to the front, helped himself to a fishing rod, and began beating the water with it.

"Stop it, Gareth!" shouted Sophie.

"NO!" shouted Gareth.

Ducks flew everywhere. All the little animals waiting in the line began to scream. Mrs Squirrel got soaked.

"Here! Here's a balloon! Just take him away!" she begged.

Gareth loved his balloon. It was a
big red one. Sophie tried to tie it to the
strap on his dungarees.

"So it won't fly away," she told him.

But Gareth didn't want it tied. He wanted to hold it. He screwed up his face and took a deep breath. Sophie knew that look.

"All right," she said hurriedly. "Just make sure you don't lose it."

"NO!" said Gareth happily, and toddled off at top speed.

"That brother of yours is a pest," called Graham Frog, who was waiting in the Face Painting queue.

"You're telling me," panted Sophie, running by.

She caught Gareth just as he was helping himself to a bright yellow tractor from the Old Toys stall.

"Paws off, Gareth!" she scolded him.
"Put it back, there's a good little
bunny."

"NO!" bellowed Gareth. "Want it!
Want tractor!"

And he pulled at the cloth covering
the stall.

The cloth slipped, and Gareth sat
down with a bump, looking surprised.
Toys rained down on the grass.

"Now see what you've done!" said
Sophie crossly.

"Don't worry, Sophie," said Mrs
Badger, who was on the toy stall.
"It won't take long to pick them up."

She was right. It only took a minute, especially as Fran and Kelly Mouse kindly stopped to help.

A minute is only a short time – but it was long enough for Gareth.

Sophie put the last toy back, looked around for him....

… and he was gone!

"Gareth?" called Sophie, peering into the bustling crowds. "Where are you?"

But there was no sign of him.

Graham Frog came zooming up with his face painted as Spider Frog.

"I'm Spider Frog," he said. "I help animals in distress."

"Good. You can help me look for Gareth," said Sophie worriedly. "I'm supposed to be in charge of him, and I think he's lost."

"We'll help," offered Fran and Kelly immediately.

And the search was on.

The Mouse twins checked the
Roundabout, and Graham tried the
Bouncy Mushroom. Sophie raced back
to Hook-the-Duck, but Mrs Squirrel
hadn't seen him. Then she ran to the
cake stall, but lots of animals were

buying cakes. She couldn't get near
her Mum.

Anxiously, Sophie climbed to the top
of the Hoopla stall, and looked over
the crowds. And there, on the far side
of the playground, she saw two little
ears, poking through some brambles.

So. What had become of Gareth? Well, when he sat down so unexpectedly, he let go of his red balloon, just as Sophie thought he would. A mischievous breeze had snatched it – and he had gone toddling off in hot pursuit.

The balloon had blown into a bramble bush growing at the edge of the playground – where, of course, it went off BANG! right in his face. Poor Gareth. His lovely balloon was gone – and even worse, he couldn't see Sophie. He sat down by the brambles, buried his face in his paws, and sobbed.

He was still weeping when Sophie came running. Big fat tears plopped down on to the tiny piece of red rubber by his side.

At the sound of her voice, he looked up and a big, wobbly smile of relief spread across his grubby face.

"Oh, Gareth!" said Sophie, hugging him close. "I thought I'd lost you. Did you miss me? Were you frightened?"

"NO," said Gareth. But he held her
very tight. Then a familiar voice said:
"Ah, there you are. We've been
looking for you two."

"Oh, dad," said Sophie. "am I glad to see you!"

"How's my boy?" cried Mrs Rabbit, hurrying up with Sam and Louise. "Was he a good boy for Sophie?"

"YETH," said Gareth, beaming.

"NO," said Sophie, with feeling.

But she smiled as she said it.

Because everything was all right.

Gareth was found, dad was here, the

sun was still shining – and best of all,

she wasn't in charge!